HAUNTIQUES

Raintree is an imprint of Capstone Global Library Limited, a company incorporated in England and Wales having its registered office at 264 Banbury Road, Oxford, OX2 7DY – Registered company number: 6695582

www.raintree.co.uk
myorders@raintree.co.uk

British Library Cataloguing in Publication Data
A full catalogue record for this book is available from the British Library.

Designed by Hilary Wacholz
Original Illustrations © Capstone Global Library Limited 2017
Illustrated by Rudy Faber
Production by Tori Abraham
Originated by Capstone Press
Printed and bound in China.

ISBN 978 1 4747 2548 4
20 19 18 17 16
10 9 8 7 6 5 4 3 2 1

HAUNTIQUES

GHOSTLY GOALIE

written by Thomas Kingsley Troupe

illustrated by Rudy Faber

raintree
a Capstone company — publishers for children

My tank explodes in slow-motion on the TV screen. It's bad enough when the computer beats me, but with Hai sitting next to me and laughing, the humiliation is even worse.

"Wait, Casey, wait," Hai says, pointing at the screen as the scene replays from different angles. "It's the best when your guy totally flies out and eats a mouthful of dirt!"

"And he's on fire," I mutter. I'm ready to throw the controller out of the window.

Digi-Tanks 2: The Wreck-oning arrived in the post yesterday, a full three days after it was released. Living in a smaller town like Stonewick, we don't have shops nearby that sell that kind of stuff. I tore it open and started playing immediately. I love video games, but the sad truth is that I'm terrible.

Hai, on the other hand, is practically unbeatable. It doesn't matter what game it is, how long I've had it or the hours of practice I put in, Hai beats me every time. Take *Digi-Tanks 2* for example. Though I've had a full day of practice and Hai's never played the game, you'd never know it.

"Oh, weird," Hai says, accessing some power-up that grants his tank heat-seeking missiles. "I think I just levelled up." He blasts me into oblivion again.

I don't think Hai tries to make me feel bad for being so rubbish at games. It's not his fault he's awesome at them. He picks up the controller, learns the moves instantly and makes me look like a total newbie. It doesn't help that I have a hard time remembering which button does what.

"Another round?" Hai asks. He's nodding towards the TV.

"Yeah," I say, taking a deep breath. "Why not?"

"Cool," Hai says. He pushes the X button to get the game started. "I've got to try out the heat-seekers again."

Hai Boon has been my best friend ever since his family moved to Stonewick four years ago to open Boon's Kitchen, the only Chinese restaurant we have in town. His dad is an amazing chef. We rarely play video games at Hai's house since he's got two older brothers and two younger sisters. Trying to get at one of the TVs in his house is next to impossible.

"Okay, seriously?" I shout at the TV. I fire half a dozen rockets at Hai's tank and completely miss. "How are you making your tank roll like that?"

"Ancient Chinese secret," Hai says, slamming my digital tank with a barrage of missiles. I pull back behind a wall, so my tank has a chance to recoup and reload. I'm literally ten seconds in, and half of my armour has already melted off. Stupid game.

"Casey," my mum calls from the kitchen. "Is Hai planning on staying for supper?"

I turn my head for a second to answer her, a fatal mistake. Hai attacks with another swarm of missiles, and my tank explodes into a gazillion pieces.

"I hope not," I answer.

Hai play-punches me in the shoulder and sets his controller down. "I can't tonight, Mrs Willis. My parents need some help at the restaurant, so I'll probably just eat there."

Sometimes when my family goes to Boon's for dinner, Hai is our host and leads us to our table. No one else in middle school has a job, but Hai doesn't seem to mind that he has one. Since it's his family's place, child labour laws don't count. It's funny seeing him pass out menus and acting all professionally.

"Okay," Mum says. "Casey, honey, can I talk you into running to the shop for me?"

"Yeah, sure," I say. "I can do that."

I power down the game console and toss my controller aside. I don't even worry about saving my game. Why would I want to save that kind of progress?

"I should get going anyway," Hai says. He stands up to stretch.

My mum gives me a list, and I tell Hai I'll walk part way with him. It's winter, so I bundle up with a heavy coat, hat and gloves. Hai refuses to wear a winter hat. He thinks it'll mess up his hair.

Like I said, Stonewick is a small town. Really small. Boon's Restaurant is just a few minutes from my house. Before I was born, the town was in pretty bad shape. Places went out of business, and a lot of people moved away, which left a lot of houses empty for a long time. Some new people have moved in and renovated the old houses. A few businesses have come into town. We even have a Creamy King ice cream shop. My dad grew up in Stonewick and says it's nicer here than it used to be.

As we walk into the town centre, I see the usual places: Food Basket Convenience Store, Dolly's Diner, Mitchell & Sons Hardware shop and the library. As we walk, a big red SUV pulls up to an abandoned and boarded-up building. Large pieces of tacked-up plywood cover the windows, the signs, everything. The wood is totally faded from being out in the sun for who knows how many decades.

My dad told me it used to be a general store, back when the shop first opened. He said that no other business owners tried to buy or update the run-down old place. The top floor looks like a flat that no one has lived in for forever. As long as I've known about it, the place has just been empty, old and creepy.

When a rear door of the red SUV opens, a girl about my age climbs out. She squints in the sun and checks things out. A second later, another girl who looks the same – except with glasses – hops out from the other side. She slips a bit on the icy pavement before she falls down on her rear end.

"Wow." Hai laughs. "She totally wiped herself out."

The girl dusts herself off as Hai and I watch from the corner. The driver and passenger doors open and people who might be their parents slip out. Their skin seems tanned, and they're not exactly dressed right for the weather.

"Visitors?" I say to Hai.

"Should I go and ask them?"

"No, no," I whisper.

I know it's not polite to stare or whatever, but I watch as the man opens the back of the SUV and pulls out a crowbar. With a couple squeaks, he pries a big panel of plywood off the front of the shop as the others watch. The woman and the clumsy girl clap once the old front door is exposed. The other girl just crosses her arms.

Squinting in the winter sun, I can make out some lettering behind the pried-off panel that was probably painted on the front door's window a million years ago.

Red's General Store, it says.

"I don't think they're visiting," I whisper. "I think they're here to stay."

After a few minutes, the man, woman and girls disappear inside the old shop. Though I can't even imagine what the inside of that place is like, I'm pretty sure it was boarded up for a reason. My imagination kicks in as I start to think about the types of dead critters, human bodies or zombies in there. I might need to lay off the video games.

Hai nudges me. "Casey," he says. He snaps his fingers in front of my eyes. "Mate."

I blink twice and realize I'm staring at the old general store. Maybe I'm waiting for them to scream in horror or come running out. Maybe they'll try desperately to tack the wooden panel over the door again.

Somewhere, deeper in the older building, one of the new people turns on a light. A dim, eerie glow lights up the door.

"Yeah, okay," I say finally. "We should go."

"You think they're moving into that old dump?" Hai asks.

"I don't know," I say. "They'd be crazy to. That place seems spooky."

"Just because it's old?" Hai asks. "News flash, Casey. This whole town is old."

On High Street, we say goodbye, and Hai crosses the street to his dad's restaurant.

I take a left and cross High Street to get to the Food Basket. I look for the stuff mum needs for dinner. Since our family has shopped at the little grocery shop forever, I find everything easily enough and head back home.

Of course, on my way back, I watch to see what the new people are up to. The boot of their SUV is open, revealing a few jammed-in suitcases.

Maybe they're just on holiday, I think as I walk by. *Nah, that can't be right. Their dad pulled the boards off the front door.*

Just then, the front door opens and the twin without glasses catches me staring in her direction. Totally busted, I pretend to be looking anywhere else: sky, trees, streetlights. I'm sure I look ridiculous. I hustle on past and don't bother to glance back.

◆

"Hey, Dad," I ask, sitting down to eat our lasagne dinner. "What's happening with that old general store?"

"Red's?" My dad says. He's dumping some lettuce into a bowl with the oversized wooden fork and spoon. "That boarded-up building?"

"Yeah," I say. "Some family was poking around in there tonight."

"Maybe someone is finally buying that place," Mum answers for him, cutting the lasagne into perfect rectangles. Some sauce squirts up on her finger, and she winces before wiping it with her napkin.

"It's been closed forever," Dad adds. "I was probably your age when it went out of business. The guy that ran the place, old Red, was a character. He got a little strange with old age. When the business was shut down, he boarded the place up but continued to live in the flat above the shop."

"Strange?" I ask. I shake some cheese onto the slab of lasagne Mum has plopped onto my plate. "Like, what do you mean?"

Dad pauses a moment as if he's trying to remember. Either that or he's about to make up something funny. It's hard for me to tell when he's kidding or not.

"He would snap at people when they walked by," Dad says. "Mean ol' geezer. Seems he blamed people in town for his shop closing. He'd say stuff like, 'Look what you did to me!'"

I think about that as I start in on my lasagne. Sure, I know Stonewick ran into hard times in the past, but could he really blame the people who lived there? It wasn't their fault if the jobs went away. Without jobs, there wasn't money. Without money . . . well, everyone knows how that works.

"What ever happened to him?"

"I'm not sure," Dad says. "Maybe he died up in that flat, alone."

"David!" Mum snaps. "Don't say things like that. Casey will get nightmares again."

"No, I won't, Mum," I say. But to be honest, the thought that some old rotted-out skeleton lived in the flat above the shop is kind of creepy.

"Well," Mum says, spearing a forkful of salad, "whatever those people are doing with that old place, I'm glad it's something. That old shop is an eyesore. And it's right in the middle of town. Like a wart."

"C'mon, Mum," I mutter. "I'm trying to eat over here."

It makes me wonder, though. *What are they doing in that old place?*

It's Monday, and I'm back at school. Mrs Hennes is standing in front of the class during tutor group. As usual, it's taking her five minutes to get everyone to stop talking and get in their seats when the girls from the SUV push through the door and look around like they're lost or something.

"Hi, girls," Mrs Hennes says with a brimming smile. "Stand up here for a moment, won't you, please?"

Except for the glasses, it's hard to tell the girls apart. The twin who caught me staring at the shop stands there with her arms folded while the one with glasses stares at her feet.

"Class, I'd like to introduce you to two new students who will be joining us this year," Mrs Hennes says. She points to the crabbier of the twins. "This is Beth Markle, and –"

"Actually, I'm Beth," the twin with glasses says, looking up. "And that's Liz."

"I'm sorry," Mrs Hennes says, shaking her head. "I knew I'd mess that up. This is Beth and Liz Markle."

I can't stop staring at the twins. I wonder what kinds of creepy stuff they'd already found in the shop. I wonder if they've run into Red's dead old body. I wonder if they like video games.

Trisha Reep raises her hand. Like always.

"Yes, Trisha," Mrs Hennes says. "What is it?"

"I have a question," Trisha says, which is pretty obvious since she raised her hand. "So if you're Liz and you're Beth, don't you have the same name? Elizabeth?"

A few classmates murmur as if they hadn't thought of that. I admit it, I didn't. I've been too busy simply staring, wondering what their story is. It isn't often that we get new kids at school.

"Actually Beth is short for Bethany," Beth says, fidgeting with her glasses.

"So what's Liz short for?" Hai asks.

I'm getting warm with embarrassment even though I didn't ask the question.

Liz gives Hai a dirty look. "Lizard," she says.

"Actually," Beth says, "Liz's full name is Lizette. She doesn't like it much, though."

I find myself staring at Beth. She seems pleasant and patient while Liz seems like she has a quick temper.

"Anyone else?" Mrs Hennes asks. She checks the room for raised hands.

"Where are you from?" Jenny Wildred asks.

"Northern California," Beth says and smiles.

"Where it's warm," Liz adds.

"I have another question," Hai says. "Are you the kind of twins that feel pain when the other is hurt?"

"My head hurts from all of these dumb questions," Liz says. "Does yours, Beth?"

"No," Beth says, touching her forehead. "It's fine."

"How about superpowers," Hai says. "Any special abilities we need to know about?"

"None that I know of," Beth says. She adjusts her glasses.

"I kind of wish I had super powers right now," Liz says. She folds her arms and stares Hai down like he's some sort of arch villain.

I'm ready to hide underneath my desk. I have to say something to get Hai to stop asking such dumb stuff. I raise my hand.

"Casey Willis?" Mrs Hennes asks, calling on me. "You have a question?"

"Did you move into the old general store?" I ask.

Liz glares at me and smirks. "You should know," she says. "Weren't you watching us from across the street?"

My heart stops, and I can feel everyone staring at me. I don't know what to say. My ears basically burst into flames.

"Well, we're always excited to get new students in Stonewick," Mrs Hennes says, saving me. "Sometimes we forget our manners. Okay, girls. Go ahead and take your seats."

Mercifully, the Markle twins sit on the other side of the room. I don't know what it is, but they fascinate me. Especially Beth. Maybe it's just because I've known all the girls in my class since we were in nappies, and they almost seem like sisters to me.

But Beth Markle is different. In a good way.

So I might have a crush on Beth Markle. Big deal. I mean, who wouldn't? When she smiles, it's like sunlight blasting through a blizzard. Her bright blue eyes sparkle, even behind her glasses and her long, brownish-blonde hair is like strands of gold, cascading down her head and past her almost angelic face. The best part? She seems nice, but kind of shy. If I was even a little brave, I'd go over and talk to her, maybe sit with her at lunch. That kind of stuff isn't easy for me. I don't know if it's a small town thing, but at my school the minute you do something different, people talk. And when people talk, word gets around fast. The last thing I need is for some big mouth to ruin everything and scare her off. But mostly? It's because I'm chicken.

Liz, meanwhile, seems like she'd kick you in the stomach just for looking at her wrong. Liz, I'm learning, is amazing at sports. The other day we played dodge ball in PE. With everyone on our side out except Liz, Joe Stewell wound up and sailed a ball at her, hard and fast. Joe, who is easily the biggest boy in our year, doesn't care if you're a boy or a girl. I was pretty sure Joe's throw was going to knock Liz off of her feet. Liz didn't even flinch. She slid across the floor on her knees towards the ball and caught it, knocking Joe out of the game. Without even gloating, she got up and fired. The ball hit Ryan Preston in the stomach so hard that it practically folded him in half. Seconds later, Liz had mopped up the entire opposing team.

In no time at all, the Markle twins are beginning to fit in. I still don't dare talk to Beth because I don't know what I'm doing when it comes to girls. I never cared much about the whole boyfriend/girlfriend thing before now.

I also notice that the general store is completely free of boards. Beth and Liz's parents are out in the November cold, sanding and painting the place to make it look nice. At some point they painted the word ANTIQUES in the windows with a fancy white paint, which gives it an old-style feel. It's cool to see this shop taking on a new look. Even so, I still can't help but think messing with that abandoned place was a bad idea.

Today, the Markle Twins are standing in front of the class again, this time with yellow flyers in their hands.

"Our parents are making us pass out invitations," Liz declares, acting like she'd rather be eating chalk. "They've turned that old shop into a place that sells old junk, so come and buy something." With that, Liz walks up and down the aisles and hands out the bright sheets of paper.

Beth smiles and shakes her head a little. "What Liz means to say," she says, "is that the Markle family would like to invite you to the grand opening of our antique shop, Days Gone Buy. We've just opened today, so if you want to stop by after school and say hi, that would be great."

I nod.

I know I would love to stop by and say hi. Well, I'd probably stop by, anyway. I'd have to see how things went before saying hi.

"Here's your chance," Hai whispers from the seat next to me. He waves his yellow flyer back and forth.

"Seriously," I say, pretending like he's being ridiculous. "You should keep quiet."

Liz comes past and shoves a flyer up under my nose.

"Here," she blurts. I smile, but inside I think, *Besides looking alike, how is it possible that you're Beth's twin?*

I study the flyer. It's printed to appear as though it came off of an antique printing press with old-style letters declaring the GRAND OPENING! There's a picture of the shop that looks like it might have been taken back in the 1930s or whenever business was booming for Red's General Store.

"Free popcorn," Hai says. "You like popcorn, Willis."

"Yes, Hai," I say with a sigh. "I like popcorn."

"And Beth Markle," he whispers.

"I don't like you any more," I whisper back. "Knock it off, mate."

Hai smiles, and I can't keep my face all clenched up and mad. That's why I like the guy, I guess.

It shouldn't surprise anyone to know I'm heading for the Days Gone Buy grand opening. Maybe I sort of went overboard by walking over right after school, but here I am. Hai didn't want to go at all, but I made him. I wasn't going in there alone.

"Whatever you do," I say, "please don't embarrass me."

"C'mon," Hai replies, acting like he's hurt. "Why would I do that?"

We walk up to the front entrance. I notice that they have kept the words Red's General Store on the front door. The sign they have put above the front door is pretty cool, too. They've mismatched each of the letters in Days Gone Buy to look like they came from old signs and things. Pretty clever. I push open the front door, and a little bell at the top of the door jingles.

The shop is amazing. Old glass cases that were probably once part of the general store

are now filled with all kinds of old stuff. Near the back is a section with a load of antique plates and old metal cans that food was sold in once upon a time. Towards the front is an old baby's pram. An old wagon with a few creepy dolls in it marks the antique toy section.

"This place is crazy," says Hai. Like me, he's trying to see everything at once.

"Look at all the games," I say. They have board games that look ancient and boring, but the boxes are pretty cool with classic retro illustrations on them. Hai turns the handle on a semi-rusted jack-in-the-box until a creepy clown pops out. I look at a box full of old army dolls, one of which is missing his trousers.

"Hi, guys," a voice greets us from behind. I don't even have to see who said hi to us to know who it is. My heart is suddenly beating faster than I thought was possible. I spin around to see Beth Markle.

"Oh," I say. "I mean, hi. Yeah."

Hai has mysteriously disappeared to wander around the shop, leaving me with Beth. Idiot.

Beth has her hair pulled back into a ponytail, and she looks cute. "See anything you like?" she asks.

As a matter of fact, I do. But I keep my mouth shut about that.

"This . . . this is a cool shop," I say, fighting off the sudden urge to flee.

Beth turns and knocks a rack of old postcards over, scattering them on the wooden floor. A gentleman would help a lady when she drops something, but I'm frozen in place. I'm too scared, I guess.

As she picks them up, Liz comes over. "Mum wants to meet your friends," Liz says, talking about Hai and me like we aren't there, which is partially true. Hai is busy looking at old sports equipment.

I've barely said a word to Beth, and now I'll be meeting Mr and Mrs Markle? "Hello," Mrs Markle says. Her hair is kind of messy and she's wearing an old T-shirt and ripped jeans. "What's your name?"

"I'm Casey Willis," I say. "And this is . . . "

"Hai Boon," Hai says, coming over. "Hi."

"That's a lot of hi's," Mrs Markle says with a quick wink. I'm just glad Hai smiles and nods. He's heard that joke way too many times.

"Casey was the kid staring at us that first day we got here," Liz adds.

"I get it," Beth says, shutting Liz down with three words. "We're new people in a small town. Plus we're kind of weird."

"Yeah," I say, which comes out wrong. Now Beth is going to think I agree that her whole family is weird.

"It was good to meet you, Casey," Mrs Markle says. She's shaking my hand like I'm some sort of adult.

"Thanks," I say. "You, too." I look over at Beth who is smiling at the floor. Was it something dumb I said? Probably.

"Please be sure to let your parents know about us, okay?"

"I will," I promise. "For sure."

Less than a week after the Days Gone Buy grand opening, I'm thinking it's not a coincidence that the Markle family moving into town has set the weirdness into motion.

It's a Saturday in early December, and Hai and I are out in his front garden, digging in the snow. His mum convinced us to help his little sisters build a snow fort, but what this means is that his sisters Lan and Ling are in the house watching from the window while we do all the work.

As I dig the trench, Hai is packing all the extra snow up around the hole to make a wall. We fortify the fort by pouring cold water on the wall, which turns the snow to slick ice in mere seconds. We want the thing to be indestructible.

"My ears are freezing," Hai says, covering his ears with his gloved hands.

"Maybe you should wear a hat," I say, though I know he won't.

"You want me to look like a dork like you?" says Hai. "No thanks."

A sudden crash of glass makes us both jump. Something small and black shoots out of the window of his neighbour's house, and we both instinctively hit the ground, preparing for an explosion.

"Okay," I say, pushing myself up onto my knees. My heart races as I quickly glance around. "What was that?"

Hai stands up and scans the yard. He peers over the icy wall of the snow fort and points. "There," he says.

I stand up too and walk to the trench to look over the wall. Sitting there in the footprint-packed snow is an old-looking hockey puck.

The front door of his neighbour's house opens. An older guy wearing pyjama bottoms and a pair of boots comes outside and stomps through his snowy front garden. "Hey," he shouts, pointing at us. "Did you boys throw a snowball through my window?"

Hai and I stare at each other. We hadn't made any snowballs yet, let alone thrown one.

"No, Mr Preese," Hai says. "But I think a hockey puck came out of your window."

To help Hai with his defence, I point to the hockey puck wedged into the snow. Mr Preese squints as if trying to see the puck. I clomp around the wall and pick it up. Hai follows me as I walk towards his neighbour.

"See?" I say.

"That's impossible," Mr Preese blurts. "I'm the only one at home."

"Is this yours?" I ask, inspecting the puck. It has some markings I can't read under the flecks of ice on the surface. "It seems kind of old."

Mr Preese takes the puck from me. "I just bought it from the new antique shop. It's like the kind we used at school back when I was a kid. But how in the world . . . "

His voice trails off as he walks over to look at his house. Mr Preese surveys the hole in the window. It's about twice the size of the puck.

"There's glass outside in the snow," I say, pointing. "Which means it came from inside."

"Were you practising your hockey shot or something?" Hai asks. "If I did that indoors, my parents would ground me."

Mr Preese curses under his breath and storms off towards the front of his house, disappearing inside.

"Okaaaaaaay," Hai mumbles. "Well, he's just as friendly as ever."

"Yeah, nice," I reply. "He just broke a window playing hockey in his house and actually tried to blame us for it."

We look at each other and shrug.

Adults. They're weird sometimes.

Since we're mostly finished with the fort, we decide to head to my house to play some games for a bit. As we walk down the steps and head for the pavement, I hear another crash of glass.

I turn toward Mr Preese's house in time to see a hockey puck hit the pavement about five feet ahead of us.

"Okay," I say. "What is he doing? This is getting ridiculous."

Now another one of Mr Preese's windows is completely shattered. I pick up the puck and take my glove off. The puck is ice cold in my hands. Which it should be, since it's winter and the puck had just landed in the snow. But it's not like that. This puck is more like make-you-shiver-instantly cold. Cold as if frozen from the inside, and it makes my own insides shiver. I bring it over to Mr Preese who is at an obvious loss for words.

"Will you boys come in here?" Mr Preese asks from his doorway. "I need you to help me understand what's happening."

I know you're not supposed to go into a stranger's house, but in a town like Stonewick, there aren't really any strangers. Everyone knows everyone, and this is Hai's neighbour. Mr Preese opens the door and leads us upstairs. We're standing in front of a built-in bookshelf where he has stuff displayed.

"I put it here," Mr Preese says and points to the shelf where he's displayed old baseballs, football helmets, and an autographed baseball bat. "Right in this spot. When I turned around for a second, my window shattered."

"Okay," Hai says. "I totally believe you."

I totally don't believe him. "Maybe put it in a drawer," I suggest.

"Yeah," Mr Preese says and nods. He follows my advice and pulls open a nearby desk drawer and drops it on top of some papers and pens. Once the puck is in, he slides the drawer closed.

"There," I say. "Problem solved." Truthfully, I don't know if that will solve the problem. "Where did you get the puck, Mr Preese?" I ask.

"That new shop in town," says Mr Preese. "They sell old junk . . . used to be Red's General." He's snapping his fingers, trying to remember.

"It's called Days Gone Buy now," says Hai.

Mr Preese ignores Hai and looks at his windows. "Must be a magnetic force," he says.

His explanation makes no sense to me. Maybe he's messing with us or something, though I'm not sure why he would do that.

As Hai and I turn to go, I hear the scrape of something wooden. We both turn and watch as the drawer slowly opens all by itself. I can't believe what I'm seeing.

The puck pops out of the drawer, lands on the floor, and rolls, stopping at our feet.

"Take it!" Mr Preese shouts. "Get it out of here! That thing is cursed!"

I pick up the hockey puck again. Before I can ask Mr Preese what he means by "cursed", he is shooing us out of the house. Within seconds, Hai and I are standing on his front steps. We're both staring at each other, and I'm holding the puck.

"What are we supposed to do with that?" says Hai. "Neither of us even plays hockey."

I know he's trying to make a joke out of the situation. It's funny, and it's true. We play baseball in the spring and summer. Hockey isn't our game. But that's beside the point.

"There is something seriously wrong with this hockey puck, Hai," I say. "I mean, we both just saw it move on its own! What's going on?"

Hai shrugs his shoulders.

"He bought it from the antique shop," I say, looking at the puck. "Maybe we should let the Markles know there's something strange going on with it."

Hai laughs. "You're hilarious, Willis," he says. "You just wanna see your girlfriend."

"She's not my girlfriend," I say.

"Well, you want her to be," Hai says. "Admit it."

I shuffle down Mr Preese's icy front path and turn left on the pavement. "You coming?" I ask. The frigid hockey puck feels almost electric in my hand.

The little bell above the door at Days Gone Buy jingles when I come inside. A few customers browse through the old stuff.

"What're you guys doing back here?" a gruff voice asks to our right. I turn and see Liz Markle arranging old cameras on a display table.

Beth is on her knees, sweeping some fluff into a dustpan. She stands up and bangs her head on the table and knocks a camera over. Luckily, it doesn't break.

Before I can ask if Beth is okay, Liz groans, "Holy cow! Could you be any clumsier, Beth?"

Beth rubs her head and seems a little embarrassed to find both Hai and I standing here. "Hi, guys," she says.

I nod but don't say anything. I'm not sure why my motor mouth stalls whenever she's around. Thankfully, Hai's never runs out of petrol.

"So," Hai says, "my neighbour bought this hockey puck from you guys, and there's something wrong with it." He plucks the puck out of my hand.

"No refunds," Liz snaps. She adjusts the cameras' price tags, so they're more visible.

"I don't think Hai's neighbour is looking for a refund," I counter, glaring at Liz.

Hai and I explain what happened and both of the Markle twins stand there like they don't know what to say.

"Are you serious, Casey?" Beth asks, gazing right into my eyes.

I nod.

"It's true," Hai says. "Mr Preese acted like he'd seen a –"

"Let me see that," Liz interrupts. She reaches over and snatches the old hockey puck out of Hai's gloved hand. As soon as she has her bare hands on it, her surly expression changes to one of surprise.

"Cold, right?" I ask.

"Yeah," Liz says, tossing it back and forth in her hands. "What's the deal? It feels like I could get frostbite from this thing."

"It's weird," I say in agreement. "I mean it was outside, but it shouldn't be that cold."

"Can I see it?" Beth asks.

Liz hands the puck to Beth, and the moment it touches her fingers, her face changes.

"Oh," Beth whispers. It's like she's looking at us but seeing right through. I'm pretty sure if I waved my hands in front of her face, she wouldn't blink.

"Are you okay?" Hai asks.

"Something's wrong here," Beth whispers. "I don't know how to explain it."

For a moment, I wonder if maybe the two of them are playing some sort of joke on us. But Liz's eyes are wide, giving the impression that she's as baffled as we are. Beth starts breathing

faster, like someone is chasing her, but all she's doing is standing in the shop, holding the puck.

"Gordon," she whispers.

"Wait," I say. "What? Who's Gordon?"

Beth drops the puck and stumbles back a step or two.

Liz is speechless and stares at her twin for a moment like she's caught off guard or something. She starts to say something but then doesn't.

"Okay, weirdo," Liz says as she picks up the puck. I can tell by the way she flinches that the puck is still ice cold. "So what does this neighbour want anyway?"

I shrug. "Maybe an explanation as to why this hockey puck has a mind of its own? I don't know. Where did you guys get it from?"

"Not sure," Liz says. "Beth, where did Mum and Dad find this?"

Beth exhales as if she's just coming out of her hypnotic trance or something. She studies the three of us as if she can't remember how we'd got there.

"Hello?" Liz calls. "Beth, come in. Over."

"Sorry," Beth gasps. "I'm not sure what just happened to me."

Liz asks again where the hockey puck was from.

"The cellar," Beth says. "I'm pretty sure it was with all of the other stuff down there."

I'll be the first to admit I'm not at all that excited to go into the cellar of the antique shop. My afternoon has already been weird enough, thanks. But here we are, heading down some creaky wooden stairs lit with just a few bulbs on strings. It smells old and musty, kind of like my grandma's cellar. When Liz turns the lights on at the bottom of the steps, I can't believe what I'm seeing.

For as much stuff as the Markles have on their main shop floor, the cellar is loaded with three times as many things. Everywhere I look, antiques sprawl. Old clothes, dolls with empty eyes, an ironing board, rusty metal toy cars, a rusted tricycle with a broken back wheel, a dented globe, a silent grandfather clock, a dusty wall mirror, a faceless mannequin with a half sewn shirt on it.

"You guys brought all of this for the shop?" Hai asks, pretty much taking the words out of my mouth.

"No," Liz replies. "This was all here when my parents bought this old dump. We had no idea there was so much stuff down here. But since this was part of the property, now we own all of this junk."

"Wow," I say. It's like the cellar is flooded with antiques. Narrow paths cut in between the rows and rows of antiques.

"My parents thought we could sell some of these items, too," Beth says. "The guy that owned the place was a collector, I guess."

"More like a hoarder," Hai jokes, poking around. "A lot of the stuff here is . . . like, seriously random."

As bizarre as the cellar is, it still doesn't explain why the hockey puck is throwing itself out of windows. I take the puck from Liz and can feel that it's no longer cold. It's room temperature again, which is strange. I flip the puck over to see if I can read anything that may be printed on it. I squint and look everywhere but find nothing.

"Beth," I say, staring at the puck. Somehow it's easier to talk to her when I'm not face to face with her. "You said the name Gordon upstairs. Do you know why?"

"I did?" Beth says. She looks over at her twin sister as if she's afraid Liz will snap at her. "Maybe it was his hockey puck."

Hai sets down the toy ray gun he's holding. He walks over to Beth and looks at her in a completely different way.

"How would you know his name?" Hai asks. "Are you a psychic or something?"

The entire cellar is quiet as Beth seems to try and figure out a way to answer Hai.

"No," she says in a cautious whisper. "I'm not sure what I am."

"How come that puck isn't flying around any more?" Liz asks once we're back upstairs. "Other than it being ice cold, it doesn't seem all that strange to me."

"Maybe if we leave it alone, it'll do something," I suggest.

I set it down on the floor of the shop and walk away. I head towards the old toys section the Markles have set up. I brace myself, expecting a window to shatter or something.

Nothing happens. Music plays from an old radio up near the front counter. A couple of minutes later, the puck remains stone still. I never said it was a great idea.

"I think we're getting too excited here," Liz says. "The puck was cold, and Beth got day-dreamy and said something weird. I'm used to this, guys, and I've got better things to do."

I'm guessing she doesn't believe there's something strange about the puck, and I don't care either way. Liz heads for the stairs that lead up to the flat above the shop.

I know what Hai and I saw. If Liz doesn't want to help us figure it out, that's just fine. I bend down to pick up the puck. It feels kind of cold again, which doesn't make any sense at all since the shop is nice and warm inside, but I don't bother saying anything about it.

"Maybe we should try to figure out who Gordon is," I suggest. I'm not quite ready to give up. I can't help but notice that Liz, who just said she had "better things to do," hasn't wandered very far away.

Hai sighs like he's thinking he might have better things to do, too. "So even if we figure out who Gordon is, what're we going to do?" Hai asks. "Return the puck to him? Ask him why it's got a mind of its own?"

I turn the puck in my hand. The lettering, which is scratched-off, is tricky to decipher, but slowly I begin to make some sense of the faded and cracked printing. "Stonewick High School," I read aloud.

Everyone stares at me like I've got something stuck in my teeth. I hold the puck up as if I'd just made some sort of breakthrough. Mostly because I don't want our little team to break up.

"We have a name and a location," I say, as if spelling it out for everyone. "We can try and look this guy up."

Beth smiles and pushes her glasses up higher on her nose. I don't bother to ask her why she's smiling like that, but I'm hoping it's because she's finally decided that I'm brilliant and irresistible.

"That old school has been closed for probably, like, thirty years," Hai says.

He's right. Stonewick High School was shut down when the town was in really bad shape. When I asked, my parents explained that with so many families moving away, there weren't enough students in town to keep the two high schools. Since then, all older kids go to Connor High School a half hour away. Now, the old school is a just a big empty reminder of our town's tougher times.

"How are we supposed to find this Gordon bloke?" Hai asks.

"A yearbook," Liz says from the steps, followed by a sigh. She can't pretend she's not hooked on finding out more. "Maybe he was a hockey player."

I grin at the others. If they can read my face, I'm pretty sure it says: *You see?*

"Here you go, kiddos," Mrs Gulliver says.

In front of us, in the back room of our town's library, are at least fifty yearbooks. "Good night!" Hai whispers. Some of the books look older than my grandparents. All of them are dusty and smell a little funny.

"There has to be an easier way to do this," says Liz.

Stonewick hasn't spent a lot of money keeping the library up to date. The sole computer station is more like an antique exhibit. I'm not sure if it's even functional.

Mrs Gulliver, to her credit, has stuck it out for longer than anyone in the town can remember. The library is like her home, and she does the best with what she has. The place is huge for a small town library, but the card catalogue is similar to something Days Gone Buy would love to sell, and the windows are made of faded stained glass. For someone who worships books, the Stonewick Community Library is a church.

"Can we check these out?" I ask Mrs Gulliver before she scuttles away to her desk in the middle of the library.

"If by 'check them out' you mean look through them, yes," says the kindly old lady. "If you mean take them home, I'm afraid not."

"Oh, okay," I say. I wasn't sure.

"They're impossible to replace," she says. "And while I know you'd be extra careful, accidents happen." I watch as she caresses the spines of the old yearbooks as if they were her prized pets, which I guess they are.

"So where do we start?" Hai asks, pulling a yearbook off the shelf. "This one says 1947. Wow. Did they even have hockey back then?"

Mrs Gulliver helps us narrow the search by showing us twenty years' worth of yearbooks.

We bring the stacks to a table and crack them open. The black and white pictures feature students that look like overly-serious adults. The clothes they're wearing in the class photos are kind of ridiculous. The giant collars, weird patterns and big glasses remind me of my great grandma's wardrobe.

It then dawns on me. Most of the people in these yearbooks probably *are* grandparents.

By the time we've been at the library for a little under an hour, I've learned one thing: There aren't very many people named Gordon these days. Seriously. It's a pretty solid name, and I think it sounds tough and stern. I think maybe a big guy with a lot of chest hair should have a name like Gordon.

What I'm saying is, I don't know anyone named Gordon.

The problem is that there were a lot of guys named Gordon way back in the days of old. The other problem is that the sheer number of ancient yearbooks in the Stonewick Community Library is starting to overwhelm all of us.

"This is impossible," Liz mutters, flipping to the end of the yearbook she's paging through. "We don't know Gordon's last name or even what year he went to school. Using the index is a complete waste of time."

I hear Mrs Gulliver shush us from her desk near the front of the library.

"We're the only ones in here," Liz whispers, raising her eyebrows.

"That's true," I say. "But I think she's trying to read."

Hai flips through another yearbook and stops somewhere in the middle. He holds up the page to show me what he's found. It shows a number of old grainy pictures . . . of a football team.

"Wrong sport, genius," I remind him. "We need hockey."

"Yeah, but check out the shorts," Hai says, shaking his head and grimacing. "They look like they're wearing ladies bloomers."

Beth giggles. I sigh. Liz gets up and goes over to the old computer and turns it on. She seems like she's ready to slip into a boredom coma. This isn't going well.

I take my time, poring through each of the books in a concentrated attempt to find our Gordon. I search through each class one by one, and I stop every so often to jot down the year and the full name of the Gordons I find. Gordon Harvey, Gordon Anderson, Gordie Smalls, Gordon Pruitt.

I add more Gordons and Gordies to my list. Then I try and find any hockey team pictures to see if any of the Gordons on my list are on any of the teams. Out of all of the yearbooks we're looking through and all of the Gordons I find, it turns out there were a whopping five Gordons who played hockey.

I open up the five yearbooks and spread them out. When I glance up, I notice that Beth has that look in her eyes again. She clutches the edge of the library table and gapes up at the ceiling. It's sort of scary, as though she's about to have a seizure.

The air in the library feels chilly and heavy.

Something's definitely changed.

"He's here," Beth whispers.

I keep my eye on the puck, almost expecting it to zip across the library and break one of the old stained glass windows. "Who's here?" I ask. "Gordon?"

"I . . . I don't know," Beth says. Her lips pucker like she's just eaten a whole bag of super sour sweets. "My arms . . . " Beth holds out her arms, and I can see her tiny blonde hairs standing on end, her skin raised in goosebumps. Her breaths come out in gasps.

"He touched my hand," Beth whispers.

"Who did?" Liz asks, from behind the thick computer monitor. "Casey did?"

"I didn't!" I blurt, which makes me look totally defensive. I don't think Beth notices, though. Her head is somewhere else.

Suddenly, the hockey puck, which sits on the end of the table near the yearbooks, starts to move. Hai is watching it, too. I hold my breath.

"Are you hearing something?" Liz asks.

Beth nods. Her face locked into an odd sort of concentration.

"Do you think it's Gordon's ghost?" Hai asks. He's the first to actually say out loud what we're all probably thinking: that what we might be dealing with is a spirit.

Beth exhales. "He doesn't like that," she says in an airy whisper. "Don't call him that."

The hair on my arms stands up now. For as much as I think I like Beth, she can be kind of creepy.

Hai whispers, "Maybe he got hit in the head with the hockey puck and died. That could be why he's haunting the puck."

As soon as Hai says it, the puck rises up and shoots across the library like a hard-struck slap shot. It strikes a book in the kid's section, sending a couple of other picture books crashing to the ground.

"Stop talking about him," Beth warns, in a frantic voice. It's almost like she thinks Hai is making fun of Gordon and his haunted hockey puck.

"Is this a joke?" Liz shouts, jumping up from her chair at the computer station. "Did one of you do that?"

Mrs Gulliver turns and shushes us again. I don't think she's noticed the fallen books. Before we know it, the puck zips across the room again, smacking into the backrest of the chair Liz had just jumped out of.

I have the urge to stand up and do something. "Gordon," I whisper. "We're sorry. We didn't mean to make you mad."

Hai blinks twice and looks at me, then glances over at Beth.

"You're talking to a gh –"

"Don't say it," I interrupt him, feeling every muscle in my body shake. "And yes. I'm talking to Gordon."

"Can you hear him, too?" Beth asks. She stares at me with an expression on her face that I know I'll never forget. It's like she's suddenly found someone who shares the same gift or curse that she has. Her eyes sparkle in the dim light of the library's stained glass windows.

I really hate having to tell her the truth, but now's not the time for lies. "No," I admit. "I just want him to know that we're trying to help."

Beth seems slightly disappointed by this, and for a moment, I wish I would've lied to her. Maybe she'd like me more if I say I can hear ol' Gordon clear as day. But I didn't, so . . .

"He's not upset," Beth whispers. "He's calmed down. He thinks we can help him."

"Help him how?" Hai asks. "How are we supposed to help a guy we don't even know?"

Beth takes in a deep lungful of air as if bracing for something.

Liz cries out again, making all of us jump. She backs away from the computer, knocking over the wooden chair. It clatters on the hard floor as Liz's hands cover her mouth.

"What?" I ask, holding on to the back of my own chair. "What happened?"

Liz points at the screen. Before I can even get to the workstation to see what's freaking her out, she runs off across the library and out of the front door.

I walk around to the monitor to see for myself. The screen is an old giant one that displays only green. The screen is blank, except for the three rows of letters. I look close and read what it says, over and over.

ANOTHER CHANCE. ANOTHER CHANCE. ANOTHER CHANCE. ANOTHER CHANCE. ANOTHER CHANCE. ANOTHER CHANCE. ANOTHER CHANCE. ANOTHER CHANCE. ANOTHER CHANCE. ANOTHER CHANCE. ANOTHER CHANCE. ANOTHER CHANCE. ANOTHER CHANCE.

I stand there for a moment and watch as something I can't see continues to type the words over and over again. I can hear the clacking of keys and watch invisible fingers touch the letters over and over again. Prickles of cold wash over me.

"What is it?" Hai asks.

"Gordon wants another chance," I say. As soon as the words are out of my mouth, the typing stops.

◆

Now, Mrs Gulliver is a nice enough lady, but I'm guessing we made too much noise for her taste. Though we're on the opposite end of the library from her front desk, she probably heard the chairs fall and us shouting. Now she's standing near the large print section, holding a couple books in front of her.

"What is all the commotion?" Mrs Gulliver asks. "It sounds like a professional wrestling match over here."

"Sorry, Mrs Gulliver," I say. "We got spooked and –"

"Your friend ran right out of the front door," she says. She points at the library's entrance. "Didn't even stop when I asked her to walk!"

"She's a little jumpy," Hai says, picking up the fallen chair.

"I'd ask you to leave if you can't behave, but it's almost time to close up anyway," she says. She starts to usher us out of the front door.

"Wait," I say, thinking fast. "Can we make some quick photocopies? You know, since we can't check these books out?"

"Sure," she says. "Show me what you need, and I'll run them off for you."

We wait outside while she zips off copies of the yearbook pages for us. When she comes back out with the papers, she doesn't bother to charge us for them.

"Thank you," Beth says. "I'm sorry we were so noisy."

Mrs Gulliver nods and smiles before closing the door and locking it behind her. Holding the photocopies in my hand, the three of us stand around on the front steps. I didn't know where Liz ran off to, but I guess she went back home.

"Liz really got scared," I say.

"I'm not sure what he means by another chance," Beth admits.

"Another chance at life?" Hai suggests.

Hai and I both look around, as if we expect Gordon to show up again to angrily slap the puck around the car park.

"He's not with us any more," Beth whispers.

"What does it sound like when he talks to you?" I ask, afraid of what she'll say.

"It's hard to explain," Beth says, stuffing her hands into her coat pockets. "I get little rushes of sound and parts of words. I can't always understand what he's saying."

"Were you always able to talk to . . . " I begin, picking my words carefully. "You know . . . them?"

"No," Beth says. "But I've always been more sensitive to smell and noise and stuff. My parents always say that as twins Liz and I might appear identical, but we're very different."

"No kidding," Hai says in agreement. "You guys are nothing alike. Liz is tough and seems like she could beat me up and you seem more, I don't know . . . "

I can see Beth wait for Hai to finish. She's probably curious to hear what description he'd come up with. So am I.

"Delicate, maybe?"

Beth shrugs, and I shake my head.

Hai pulls out his phone to check the time.

"I need to get home," he says suddenly. "Jeez, it's just about five."

I have to be back at my house for supper, too. It feels like we should do more, but I'm not sure what else we can do. We've narrowed down the search a bit, but even so, we still don't know how to help Gordon.

Maybe the puck is meant to be tied to Gordon forever. But why?

I'm not going to lie. I'm completely obsessed with trying to figure out what the deal is with Gordon. At dinner, I don't eat much. It takes me twice as long as usual to finish my homework because the numbers aren't registering. I'm even distracted while playing *Digi-Tanks 2*.

Late at night, I stare up at the ceiling in my darkened room. At the slightest noise, I jump. I'm convinced that Gordon's ghost decided to follow me home. If anyone should be scared, though, it's Beth. She took the puck back to the shop. I can't imagine trying to sleep with the possibility of actual voices in my head.

After lying awake for two hours, I get out of bed and head over to my desk. I sit down on my chair and click on the lamp. The photocopies of yearbook pages that Mrs Gulliver made for me lie right next to my homework. It probably didn't help to have them there while I was working on my maths homework.

I spread the pictures around and look at them. Using the captions beneath each photo, I find the Gordons and circle them with a black marker. None of them appear evil or even scary, just really old, like everyone from the past does to me. One of the Gordons wears goalie pads and looks twice as big as the others. The other four hold their sticks. One of them is missing a few teeth. I compare the Gordons and think, *Is this guy our ghost?*

I stare at the Gordon with the hole in his smile. I wonder if he caught a puck in the teeth? Would that be a reason to haunt a puck? Doesn't seem likely.

The floor in the hallway creaks, and I turn in my chair, ready to dive under my covers. My heart is beating a million miles an hour, and I'm convinced that if something is out there waiting for me, it can hear the drum solo happening in my chest.

A moment later, the bathroom light clicks on. I hear my dad yawn, and after a few moments, he flushes the toilet. I exhale and turn off my desk lamp. I climb back into bed and hop back out a second later to turn the lamp back on.

That's right. I'm in year seven, and I need a nightlight like when I was three. Whatever.

◆

When I wake up the next morning, I turn the lamp off right away. I don't want my parents to think I'm afraid of the dark. Ghosts, maybe, but not the dark.

At breakfast, I decide to run a couple of questions dealing with the supernatural past my parents. "Hey," I say, swirling the stray pieces of cereal in their milk bath. "Do you guys believe in ghosts?"

"I don't," Mum says. "But I know some people that do."

"Well, I used to think your grandpa's house was haunted," Dad says. "We even tried one of those things where you try to talk to the dead."

"A séance," says Mum over the lip of her coffee mug.

"Did it work?" I ask, setting my spoon down. "Could you hear anything?"

Dad shakes his head. "No. We were too busy messing around, making it seem like something was happening. Why do you ask?"

Both of them stare at me like I have something to reveal. Or maybe they're just preparing to tell me that there are no such things as monsters or ghosts or whatever.

"Oh, no reason," I say, finishing my orange juice. I'm not sure why I don't tell them what's going on with the Markle Twins, Gordon and the hockey puck.

They don't seem to buy it, so to change the subject I act like a lawyer in a courtroom, saying in a mock-serious voice, "No more questions, Your Honour."

◆

Two hours later, the four of us huddle up in a back room at Days Gone Buy. Like usual, Liz acts like she'd rather be anywhere else.

"So how is this supposed to work?" Liz asks, "And why am I here again?"

"I think Gordon likes to communicate with the two of you," I say, which is partly made up but just might be true. "We've only been able to get messages through the two of you."

It kind of makes sense. The ghost talked to Beth yesterday but wasn't afraid to make a message appear on the library's old computer where Liz was sitting. I have no idea what I'm doing, but I think if we're all together and calm, maybe we can at least ask Gordon to talk to us. At the very least, I hope he can let us know who he is. Then, maybe we can figure out why he's haunting the puck or why his ghost needs to stick around.

"Why don't we record the audio of this with my phone?" Hai suggests. He pulls his phone out of his pocket. "If Beth doesn't always understand what he's saying, maybe we can somehow still catch Gordon's voice."

"Hey, why not make a video while you're at it?" Liz asks. "That way we can watch it back to see how dumb we all look."

As I set the photocopies on the table, Beth touches the hockey puck. She glances up and catches me watching her.

"Are we okay?" I ask.

"He's coming," she whispers.

As soon as she says it, the air in the room

changes. It feels chillier and tighter. I can't help but feel like someone else is present. Hai holds his phone sideways, aiming it at Beth and the puck. He nods, which means, I guess, that he's recording. I sit down across from Beth. Liz sits to Beth's right, and Hai stands behind me. I clear my throat but don't know what to do or say. Good thing I don't have to.

"Gordon," Beth whispers. "I know you're here with us. Can you give us a sign?"

Before she finishes asking, the hockey puck moves a bit along the wooden table.

"We want to help you," Beth says. She has her head down slightly, which makes her hair spill down around her face, almost hiding it. I notice she's keeping her fingers on the puck. Liz gives me a wide-eyed look. Her mouth is partially open as if she's amazed by what's happening.

And then the room is silent.

"I can't understand you, Gordon," Beth whispers, shaking her head a little. "Can you show me?"

The puck slides across the table until it comes to rest on the photocopy with Gordon, the goalie, in the line-up.

"Is that you, Gordon?" Beth asks. A moment later, she looks over at each of us.

"Is it him?" I ask. I am freaking out. My heart is giving my ribs the beating of a lifetime.

Beth nods. "That's him," she says. She seems exhausted, as if talking to Gordon's ghost has taken its toll on her.

Gordon Devitt

Betty Vannouten

...Hatley

Mary Robinson   William Dyvein

COYOTES 25
COYOTES 11
COYOTES 14
COYOTES 23
COYOTES 10
COYOTES 16
COYOTES 9

top: Glenn Clark, Paul Ellis, Sean O'Malley, Gordon Williams
bottom: Tommie Wolfe, Buddy Jon Parker, Gene Andrews

I pick up the photocopy to read the name below the picture. "Gordon Williams," I read aloud. My hands shake. My fingers sweat.

"Yes," Beth says and nods. She is still talking to Gordon, but none of us can hear what he's saying. "You'll get another chance."

And just like that, our little ghost talk is over.

Liz grabs a laptop from upstairs and brings it down into the small room with us. She powers it on, and while we wait for it to warm up, I study the picture of Gordon. He's as thin as a hockey stick in his goalie pads and gear. Most of the other players smile, but Gordon Williams looks like he wants to be somewhere else.

"Another chance," I mumble, scanning at the picture. "Another chance at what?"

"He might just want to play hockey again," Liz says, staring at the laptop screen. "I know I'd miss netball if I couldn't play any more."

I shrug. It's not the worst idea, but I feel like there's something more to it. Would Gordon's ghost really stay attached to the puck just because his hockey days were over? Because, let's face it: More than just his hockey days are over – all of his days are over.

Beth takes off her glasses and rubs her eyes. "He's still talking to me," she whispers. "Saying something about trying his best."

"What was the date on that yearbook?" asks Liz

Yesterday, I wrote the year in the corner of each of the photocopies. I read them off to Liz. I also notice the team name, Coyotes, on their shirts. Liz types in keywords.

Hockey. Gordon Williams. Goalie. Stonewick. Coyotes.

Hai heads over to Liz in order to see what she has pulled up.

"There's not much," Liz says. "A couple of old photos and a newspaper archive. This could take a while."

"Why can't he just tell us?" I say. "It's like he doesn't want us to help him!"

"I'm sorry," Beth says. "I just can't understand everything he says. I . . . I think it takes a lot of his energy to communicate."

I feel bad for getting frustrated, and I'm about to apologize to Beth when Hai points at something on the screen.

"Casey," Hai shouts. "What shirt number is Gordon wearing?"

I pull the photocopy closer to me to check. "It looks like 23," I reply. "Why?"

"Come over here," Liz says.

I walk around to the other side of the table to look at an old black and white photo someone had scanned and uploaded to the internet. The quality isn't great, but it shows a group of hockey players standing around a pretty old-looking plaque.

The team isn't the Coyotes. Standing off to the side, I can see a group of old familiar faces from the Stonewick yearbooks. One of the players has his head down as if he'd been weeping. The player is wearing goalie pads. The number on his jersey is 23.

"Gordon lost the game," I whisper and stare at the table. "And I bet that was the puck."

◆

We dig a little deeper and find a few small little blurbs from the local newspapers in the giant archive. Stonewick is a small town, and the neighbouring town of Prettle is a little bit bigger. From what the article says, the game was tied, and there wasn't much time left. The centre for the Prettle High Titans fired a fantastic slap shot from mid-ice and scored the winning goal. The goalie, Gordon Williams, never had a chance to deflect it.

Another chance.

Inside my head, it sounds like a bell has gone off. I stand up from the table and clap my hands once. I have yet another idea, but this one is almost too ridiculous to even consider.

"Do you guys have any hockey sticks in here?" I ask. "Preferably not a haunted one?"

◆

It's half an hour later and we're standing on the closest thing we can find to a hockey rink. The car park of the abandoned Stonewick High School is pretty much iced over, and the snowploughs did a terrible job of keeping it clear. I guess the town thinks if no one cares about the deteriorating school, why would any one care about the car park?

In one hand, I hold an old hockey stick the Markles had for sale in their antique sporting items section. In the other, I hold the frigid puck, which feels much colder than the weather.

"What are we going to use for a goal?" Hai asks.

Good question. There isn't much that might work as a true goal, but I see a couple

of rubbish bins that could do the trick. Hai and I grab them and drag them over, positioning them in a way to resemble a hockey goal.

"You guys are creepy, you know that?" Liz asks. "What kind of town did we move into?"

I ignore her and set the puck down.

"He's here, isn't he, Beth?" I ask as I grasp the stick in my hands. I've never actually played hockey, but I know what I'm doing with a baseball bat and figure that hockey's similar enough.

"He's close," Beth says and then slips, landing on her side. I run over and help her up.

"Did he push you?" I ask. Maybe my plan is just as dumb and creepy as Liz seems to think.

"No," Beth says, brushing the loose snow from her trousers. "I'm just a bit clumsy."

I think about the first time I saw Beth and how, even then, she'd fallen down.

"C'mon, Casey," Hai calls. "It's cold out here. Take the shot!"

I turn back towards the puck. I feel everyone's eyes on me. I line up the shot, swing my arm back, and smack the ice. The stick bounces and barely taps the puck – probably the worst shot in hockey history.

The puck slides slowly towards the right rubbish bin and hits it with a dull thunk.

"Wow," Hai says. "You should stick to baseball, Willis."

"Sometime today," Liz cries. "I'm freezing!"

I try again and again. Each shot is easily worse than the last. I finally hand the stick to Hai, who takes some shots.

His aren't much better.

"Ugh," Hai moans. "Hockey. What a dumb sport."

"My fingers are going to freeze through," Liz complains. "Even through my gloves."

"You take a shot, then," Hai says, tossing her the stick. Without even looking, Liz catches it, walks up to the puck, winds up and executes a killer shot.

And that's when something amazing happens.

10

Liz's shot is pretty much perfect. Of course it is. She's the one who thinks my idea is stupid and that we're all wasting our time.

The moment her stick connects with the puck, I know it's going to end up right in the goal. The smack echoes off of the long, empty school, and the black puck is a blur, zipping about three feet off the surface of the icy car park.

As it reaches the goal's threshold, the puck's momentum stops and it hangs in midair.

And stays there.

My mouth drops open. Liz drops the stick. All four of us watch the space just in front of the garbage-can goals as the puck simply floats, suspended in mid air. It's as if someone has pushed pause on a remote control.

"He stopped the puck," I whisper finally. "Gordon, that's awesome!"

Beth cheers. Liz says "wow" about a hundred times. Hai just stands there, his face frozen in awe. I whistle like I'm at a championship game.

And then, as if it was enough, the puck drops to the ice and stays there, just in front of our rubbish-bin goal posts. Beth hugs herself with her bundled-up arms and slides across the ice towards the puck.

We all watch her a second as she nods to someone we can't see. Then, she bends to pick up the puck.

"He's gone," says Beth. She turns and smiles at us.

"So that was all he needed?" I say, thinking the whole thing through. "To prove he wasn't a terrible goalie? All these years, his spirit's been living with the guilt of losing that game."

I think about what that must be like, about what could have happened and feeling the crush of defeat when things didn't go the way Gordon had hoped. His teammates were probably upset. Gordon, naturally, would feel like it was all his fault. Who wouldn't?

While I know what it's like to sometimes have an off day in baseball, I haven't yet been in the position where the game, especially a championship game, is riding on my shoulders.

"Hey, we should get that back to Mr Preese," Hai suggests. "Tell him his puck is going to behave itself now."

I reach for the puck, and Beth puts it in my hand. I take my glove off and can already tell it feels different. There isn't that deep-rooted cold. It feels like just an ordinary puck out in the winter air.

"Gordon said thank you," says Beth.

"Seriously?" I ask.

"No," Beth says. "But I bet he would have."

I return the puck to Mr Preese, who seems a little fidgety. I notice he's put up some wood up to cover the broken glass.

"I was going to go down to that shop and give them an earful," Mr Preese says, holding the puck up. "I wanted to get my money back."

"Well, there are no refunds," Liz says.

"What my sister means to say is that if you have any further problems with your purchase, please let us know," Beth says. "I think you'll find it will stay put. And I'm sorry you had so much trouble with this."

Mr Preese grumbles his thanks and closes the door.

"Well, let's hope that's the last time that kind of thing happens," I say as we all walk down his front steps to the pavement.

"A refund," Liz mumbles. "What did he even pay for that puck? Like five dollars? Give me a break."

We stand around for a few minutes to talk about the unreal events of the day. I'm not sure anyone will ever believe us, but it all happened, I swear. Even so, we decide to keep it to ourselves. Sure, Mr Preese saw it happen, but I can't imagine telling people at school. They'll think we're all nuts.

After a while, we all go our separate ways. I feel a little crushed on my walk back home. I'll admit I liked having an excuse to talk to Beth. Just as I was feeling a little more comfortable around her, the whole thing's over. I wonder if we'll talk much at school. Maybe we won't. Not knowing makes me feel sad.

As I get to my house, I hear feet crunching through ice on the pavement. I turn to see Hai run towards me. He's holding up his phone.

"Mate!" he shouts. "You have to see this!"

Hai shows me his screen and presses play on a video. Immediately, I see Beth sitting at the table with the photocopies of the old hockey teams. I know where this is going.

As the image of Beth talking to Gordon continues to play, I watch closely.

"I can't understand you, Gordon," Beth whispers on the video. "Can you please try to show me?"

"Watch," Hai said. He sounds completely frightened and excited at the same time.

I watch as a shadowy figure appears behind Beth's chair. It's hard to make out the details, but there's definitely a smoky, hazy person shape there. I can't see any facial features or anything, but I see a faceless head on a body and arms.

"Whoa," I whisper. We'd seen the puck
fly around and stuff, but somehow this was
different. Gordon's ghost reaches for the puck
and slides it slowly across the table until it
stops at the picture of him and his team.

Hai pauses it. Gordon has one hand on
Beth's arm and another on the puck.

Holy hockey, I think. The faceless shadow
of Gordon makes my ears ring and my spine
tingle.

"Can you believe this?" Hai whispers. "This
is like the best proof ever that ghosts exist!"

I nod and feel a nervous twinge jolt through
my shoulders. Not that I doubted it before, but
this seals it. Ghosts and spirits exist, and we'd
just made contact and helped one. Though I
don't think Gordon meant to do us any harm,

it's still weird to think a ghost was swirling around us for the last few days.

"We can't show this to anyone," I say suddenly. Hai stares at me like I need to have my head cleaned out with a wire brush.

"What?" says Hai. "Why?"

I look towards the middle of town, where the Days Gone Buy antique shop is probably selling all kinds of old stuff. "Word will get around that they sell haunted antiques," I say. "I don't know. If people get spooked . . ."

"Ha ha, spooked," Hai says. "Nice, Casey."

"I'm serious," I say. "People won't buy stuff at Days Gone Buy any more. And if they don't sell anything . . . . "

Hai smiles and nods. "Yeah, okay. I get it, mate."

"What?" I reply. "I don't want the Markles to close their shop. Stonewick can't have another place go out of business."

"So I guess this has nothing to do with Beth, right?"

I sigh. He knows me too well. "Yeah, okay," I say. "But just keep quiet, all right? I don't want to scare her off."

"Scare her off?" Hai asks. "This girl can talk to ghosts and you're worried about scaring her? You're hilarious, Willis!"

He's right, of course. But still, it doesn't change the fact that I'm not sure how I'd just be able to talk with her about normal stuff. So there's a part of me that sort of hopes they sell something else haunted.

Sort of.

HOCKEY HAUNTING

Could ghosts be haunting a hockey arena?
That may be the story with Nationwide
Arena in downtown Columbus, Ohio,
USA, home of pro hockey's Blue Jackets.
The venue was built on the site where the
Ohio Penitentiary (prison) once stood. In
1930 it burned, killing 322 inmates in the
deadliest prison fire in United States history.
The prison was also home to hundreds of
executions. Some say that the centre of the
ice may be the spot where the old electric
chair was once located. Arena employees
have reportedly sensed paranormal activity
on a number of occasions over the years.

ABOUT THE AUTHOR

Thomas Kingsley Troupe was afraid
of just about everything as a kid.
Now a full-fledged adult, he's become
fascinated by the creepy, the strange and
the unexplained. In his spare time, he
investigates ghostly activity with the Twin Cities Paranormal
Society. With his own ghost squad, he's stayed in a few
haunted places, including the Stanley Hotel in Colorado,
USA, and the Villisca Murder House in Iowa, USA.

ABOUT THE ILLUSTRATOR

Rudy-Jan Faber lives and works in the
beautiful town of Leeuwarden in the
Netherlands. Whenever Rudy has some
time to spare, he loves to lock himself
up in his attic and paint with oils. After
leaving his job as a concept artist at a gaming studio, Rudy
took up his passion for book illustration. He loves it when
he can make illustrations for super spooky stories . . . or for
stories with pirates or for super spooky stories with pirates.

GLOSSARY

decipher to interpret the meaning of

deteriorate to become steadily worse

goosebumps tiny bumps that appear on people's skin when they are cold, frightened, or excited

hypnotize able to produce a state of putting someone intro a trance

mannequin form displaying the human figure, often used for displaying clothes

psychic marked by extraordinary or mysterious sensitivity, understanding, or perception

retro looking like or relating to styles from the past

séance meeting where people try to communicate with spirits of the dead

supernatural unable to be explained by science or the laws of nature

FURTHER INVESTIGATION

1. Red, who owned the general store before the Markles turned it into antique shop, kept a load of older things in the cellar. Why do you think he did that? Do you know anyone who does this?

2. Beth and Liz are twins, but other than looking alike, they're very different, right from their introduction to the class at school in chapter two. Do you know any twins? Are they alike or different? How so?

3. When Beth and Liz Markle move to town, they're the new kids. Have you ever been the new kid in town? Are you friends with anyone who has been?

4. Hai and Casey captured a ghostly image on Hai's phone. Have you ever seen or captured something strange or unexplainable on video? Compare your experience to Hai and Casey's.

5. Write a short story about a haunted sporting goods item. It could be an old shirt, pair of shoes or ball.

Uncover the mysteries of
HAUNTIQUES...